A Day with Nellie

Marthe Jocelyn

Tundra Books

For Henry, Joseph, and Jake – new cousins

Published in Canada by Tundra Books,
481 University Avenue, Toronto, Ontario M5G 2E9

Published in the United States by Tundra Books of Northern New York,
P.O. Box 1030, Plattsburgh, New York 12901

Library of Congress Control Number: 2002101726

National Library of Canada Cataloguing in Publication Data

Jocelyn, Marthe
        A day with Nellie

ISBN 0-88776-600-5

        I. Title.

PS8569.O254D39 2002   jC813'.54   C2002-900779-8
PZ7

We acknowledge the support of the Canada Council for the Arts and the Ontario
Arts Council for our publishing program.

We acknowledge the financial support of the Government of Canada through the
Book Publishing Industry Development Program for our publishing activities.

Design: Blaine Herrmann

Printed in Hong Kong, China

1 2 3 4 5 6   07 06 05 04 03 02

Is Nellie still sleeping?

Good morning, Nellie! When Nellie wakes up, the blankets are every which way. She is ready to start her day.

What will
Nellie wear
today?

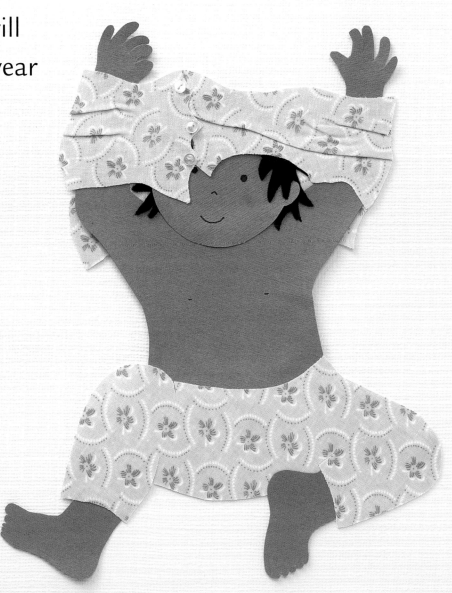

It's breakfast time. What will Nellie eat?

cold apple juice

squirty orange slices

crispy cereal o's

squishy egg

crunchy toast fingers

Will she save the best bite for last?

Nellie says hello
to her friends.

Cousin Willa

Bunny twins

Blankie

Oscar, the neighbor's cat

Donkers

Nellie in the mirror

Kiki monkey

Nellie plays indoor games all morning.

Blowing bubbles
OUT the window

Dancing IN Daddy's shoes

Riding ON the train
to the North Pole

Hiding UNDER
the castle

Nellie gets tired...cranky...stubborn...mad!

Nellie takes a nap.

All smiles again. Lunch is a picnic outdoors!

cup of lemonade

cherries

2 sandwiches

3 baby carrots

4 cookies
(Is one missing?)

and 24 ants!

Nellie swings up
to the blue sky.
What does she
see from there
this afternoon?

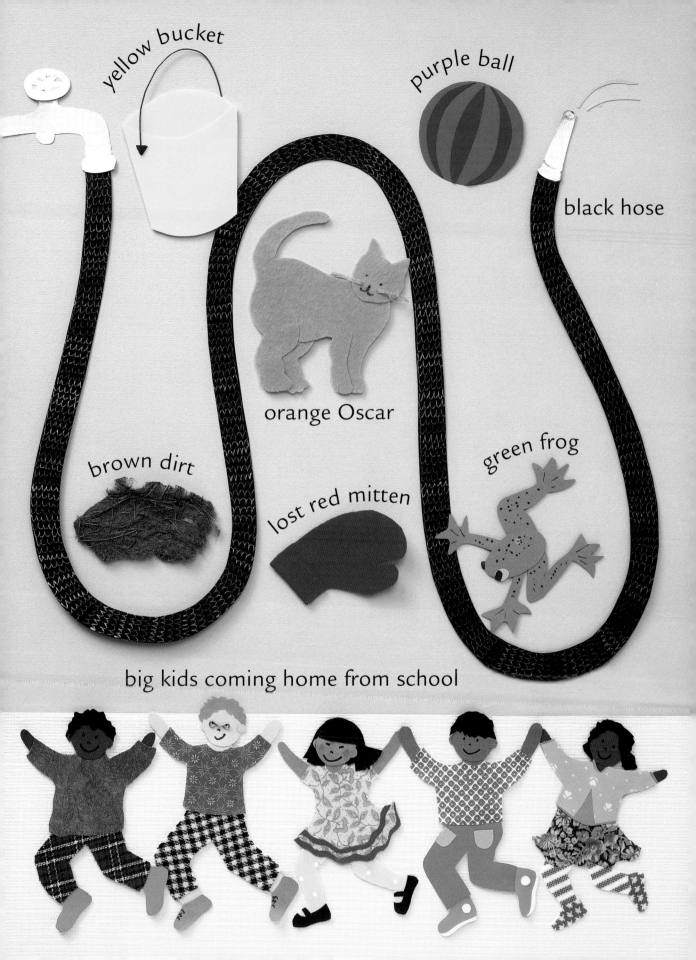

yellow bucket

purple ball

black hose

orange Oscar

brown dirt

lost red mitten

green frog

big kids coming home from school

Nellie plays teacher.

Dirt plus water
make Nellie muddy.

Soap plus water make Nellie clean.

Afternoon turns to evening. Now it's supper time.

Nellie has noodles again!

It's nearly night.
Nellie has a story
and a snuggle
with Daddy.

Time for bed.
Tomorrow is only a sleep away.
Sweet dreams, Nellie . . .